D0105832

Lucky
on the Loose

ALSO BY BETSY DUFFEY

A Boy in the Doghouse
Lucky in Left Field

Lucky
on the Loose

BETSY DUFFEY
illustrated by Leslie Morrill

SIMON & SCHUSTER BOOKS FOR YOUNG READERS
Published by Simon & Schuster
New York   London   Toronto   Sydney   Tokyo   Singapore

SIMON & SCHUSTER BOOKS FOR YOUNG READERS
Simon & Schuster Building, Rockefeller Center
1230 Avenue of the Americas, New York, New York 10020
Text copyright © 1993 by Betsy Duffey
Illustrations copyright © 1993 by Leslie Morrill
SIMON & SCHUSTER BOOKS FOR YOUNG READERS
is a trademark of Simon & Schuster.
Designed by Vicki Kalajian.
Manufactured in the United States of America

10   9   8   7   6   5   4   3   2   1

Library of Congress Cataloging-in-Publication Data
Duffey, Betsy.
Lucky on the loose / by Betsy Duffey ;
illustrated by Leslie Morrill.   p.   cm.
Summary: While George is at camp and his parents are on vacation,
his dog Lucky escapes from the kennel
where he is being boarded and disappears.
[1. Dogs—Fiction. 2. Camps—Fiction.] I. Morrill, Leslie H., ill.
II. Title.   PZ7.D876Lv   1993[Fic]—dc20   92-21421   CIP
ISBN: 0-671-86424-6

For Anna

Contents

Lucky
on the Loose

Camp Knockahoma

George looked out of the car window and watched the road signs pass. Each mile took him farther away from home and farther away from his dog, Lucky.

DILLON   20 MILES

He wouldn't look over at his father. Each mile took him closer to Camp Knockahoma. He pressed his forehead to the window and closed his eyes.

Camp had sounded like a great idea last winter when his parents had suggested it.

1

"Hey, George," his father had said as if he had just thought of it. "How would you like to go to baseball camp this summer?" His father had pulled out camp brochures.

CAMP KNOCKAHOMA

There had been wonderful pictures. Pictures designed to make children want to go to camp. Photos that made camp look like a wonderful place. There were kids playing baseball, smiling as they batted and pitched.

They were probably child models, paid to look like they were having a good time. George had figured that out too late.

It wasn't until after he signed up for baseball camp that he learned more about the summer plans. His parents were going on a sailing trip to the Bahamas. A trip without him.

In the same brown folder with the camp brochures, George found slick sailing brochures. They showed blue water and people in bathing suits waving from the deck of a gleaming white sailboat. Then George knew the truth—camp was just a way to get rid of him.

DILLON   15 MILES

Fifteen more miles. It was too late to back out. His parents were already packed for the Bahamas. His mother had been giggling all week. "I can't believe we're really going," she said over and over. "I just can't believe it! I can't believe my good luck!"

"We'll really get away from it all" had been his father's exact words.

What exactly was "it all"? George had wondered. Was he the "it all" they wanted to get away from?

He thought about Lucky, and squeezed back a tear.

Last winter he had not had Lucky. He had not known he would have a dog this summer.

4

He had had Lucky for only two months now. For two months he and Lucky had been together every minute.

They ate together. They played together. They had been like a single unit instead of two. A boy-and-his-dog instead of a boy and a dog. They had been inseparable.

No dogs were allowed at camp. At the same time that George's father was driving him to camp, George's mother was driving Lucky to Mrs. Minnie's Kennel.

Now they were separated.

DILLON   10 MILES

So far the summer had been perfect. Every day he and Lucky had played ball and had played catch with Lucky's rubber newspaper. He had taught Lucky a lot of things. To beg, to come, and not to make puddles in the house.

He would be gone for seven days. Seven days was a long time.

Would Lucky remember him at the kennel? Did dogs even have memories?

DILLON   5 MILES

He tried to picture his parents on the sailboat on the gleaming blue water. He tried to picture them sitting on the sailboat missing him, but he couldn't.

He saw the last sign:

WELCOME TO DILLON

They were here now. He pressed his forehead against the coolness of the car window and watched another sign appear.

CAMP KNOCKAHOMA

They turned into the driveway. His perfect summer was over.

The Pound

Lucky lay on the front seat of the station wagon and whined. Where was the boy's mother taking him?

Lucky had lived with his family for two months now. He knew the daily routine. The routine did not include rides with the boy's mother. He did not like things to upset the routine. The last time something upset his routine, he had ended up at the pound.

He had been happily living under the porch of an empty old house with his mother and brother and sister. His earliest memory

7

was of the warmth of his mother as he and his siblings had snuggled close to her.

The routine had been this: eat, rest, eat, rest, eat, rest. It had been a perfect routine. He had thought it would last forever.

Then one day they heard a truck. Lucky did not pay any attention to the noise at first. His mother whined. She knew. To a stray dog the sound of a truck means trouble.

Between the cracks they watched a man come over to the steps with a long stick. At the end of the stick was a noose made of black rope.

Lucky snuggled closer to his mother. She did not move but her body tensed. Lucky closed his eyes. He was glad that he was safe with his mother.

The man poked the stick between the steps a few times. Lucky's mother jumped back. Lucky fell away from her. His brother and sister fell away too. A large hand reached between the steps and lifted up his brother.

GGRRR!

His mother growled—but too late. His brother was gone. Just as quickly the hand was back and up went his sister.

GGRRR!

Lucky cowered down trying to make himself as small as possible. He had to be quiet or the man would hear him.

The hand was feeling closer. In front of him and behind him and around him and . . .

SQUEAK!

He let out the first sound of his life. Not a bark. He was too little to bark. Not a growl. He was even too little to growl. But a pitiful squeak.

The hand knew where to go.

Lucky felt the hand close around his small body.

His routine had ended.

Today, once more, something different had happened. The routine now was eat, rest, play . . . eat, rest, play . . . But today the routine had changed.

The boy had not taken him outside to play ball. He had not thrown the rubber newspaper for Lucky even once. He had not even let Lucky do his tricks.

The boy had done other things instead. He had loaded clothes and things into a blue bag. He had put the bag into the man's car. He had hugged Lucky and had even cried a little. Then the man had driven the boy away. Away without Lucky.

Lucky looked up at the boy's mother driving the car. He whined a little. The routine had changed today. And a change of routine meant trouble.

The station wagon turned off the highway. The roads were bumpy and rough. Lucky sniffed the air out the window.

Sniff. Sniff.

The air was different here. It was not the city air that he was used to. The country air smelled good. They drove a little farther down the road and made another turn.

Sniff. Sniff.

Now Lucky sniffed a different smell. Other dogs.

The smell got stronger.

He could hear another dog barking, then another and another.

ERF! ERF!

He barked back fiercely. He could bark all he wanted. He was safe in the station wagon where the other dogs could not get him.

ERF! ERF!

He called out his toughest bark. The bark that said "I'm tough!"

ERF! ERF!

He called out his "brave bark." No one could touch him now.

Soon they would be far away from *these* dogs anyway.

The car turned, drove a few more feet, and stopped. Lucky stopped barking. The car was not moving anymore.

He didn't feel so brave now. The car door opened. He didn't feel brave at all.

They were going to *this* place. This terrible place where there were other dogs that barked and sounded *big*. This terrible place that sounded just like the POUND. The POUND where dogs were taken when they weren't wanted!

He jumped down onto the floor of the car and tried to hide under the front seat.

"Come on, Lucky," said the boy's mother.

She reached in and tried to pull him out by the collar. Lucky straightened out his legs and anchored his feet in the carpet. He didn't budge.

"Come . . . on . . . Lucky," she said as she pulled.

It was no use, she could not pull him out. Lucky crawled even farther under the seat.

He listened. He heard footsteps coming toward the car. Slow, sure footsteps. The footsteps stopped.

A different hand came under the seat. A woman's hand that smelled like other dogs. A strong hand that found his collar and easily pulled him with one good firm pull.

Out he came. Out from the safety of the car. Out to where the dogs were barking. Out to the terrible place that must be the POUND.

Dear Lucky

Dear Mom and Dad,

George was staring at a white sheet of paper. It was rest time on the second day of camp. He had started a letter to his parents but he couldn't get past the first line:

Dear Mom and Dad,

He was lying on his sleeping bag on the bottom bunk of a set of metal bunk beds.

George stared at the letter. He wanted to write:

COME AND GET ME!

It really didn't matter what he wrote. They wouldn't get the letter anyway. By now they were far away on a sailboat.

He crumpled the paper and threw it away. He blinked back his tears and started another letter:

Dear Lucky,

George smiled at the words. Of course Lucky couldn't read but it made George feel better to write to him.

He licked the tip of his pencil then continued.

Dear Lucky,
    By now my parents are far away. By now you are at Mrs. Minnie's Kennel. Be glad that you are not here.
    We are slaves here. This morning I had to make up my bed, sweep out the cabin, clean the lanterns, and wash the dishes after breakfast.
    Our camp director (slave driver) is

Coach Murray. He wears a pin-striped Yankees uniform (too tight). He always has a whistle around his neck and blows it if anyone gets out of line.

He says things like:

Yes, we have dishwashers here— YOU! and

Yes, we have air conditioning here —the natural kind!

The worst thing he says is, "Drop and give me ten!" Which means we have to drop to the ground and do ten push-ups. He says this a lot.

Today we had batting practice. I hid behind the bushes beside the field and didn't bat. No one even missed me.

This morning I counted fifteen mosquito bites.

I share bunk beds with a boy named Troy. He has the top bunk. Last night he wet the bed.

I think I have poison ivy.

This is the worst day of my life. Nothing worse can happen than this.

I miss you.

Love,

George the Slave

George put the letter in an envelope and put it under his pillow. He closed his eyes and waited for rest time to be over. How was he going to get through this week?

The first day had been endless. He heard a giggle from one of the other bunks and closed his eyes tighter.

BAM!

The screen door of the cabin slammed shut. George looked up. Coach Murray had come in.

It seemed that the day could get worse after all. What now—more slave work? Coach Murray walked over to George and stopped.

The other boys got up from their bunks and gathered around George. He could feel them staring at him. Coach Murray looked upset.

George had a terrible feeling. Did Coach Murray know about batting practice?

Coach Murray cleared his throat.

"George," he said slowly.

The boys leaned even closer.

George drew in a quick breath. A hundred punishments passed through his mind. He had heard the boys talk about Coach Murray's punishments. Would he have to carry the bats? Do fifty push-ups? Or, worst of all, clean the toilets?

He looked down at his shoes and tried not to move.

"George," Coach Murray said again. Something about the way Coach Murray said his name made George look up.

Coach Murray looked grim.

"We have just had a call from Mrs. Minnie's Kennel. Your dog has escaped."

Nine boys gasped. George the loudest. He couldn't move. He just stared at Coach Murray.

"I'm sorry to bring you this news. Mrs.

Minnie at the kennel needs a picture of your dog to show to the people who are looking for him."

George stared at Coach Murray with his mouth open.

Coach Murray cleared his throat. "A picture?" he said again.

George blinked. He remembered the pictures that he had brought with him. He reached under his pillow and pulled out an envelope. He opened it and took out two pictures of Lucky.

The first was Lucky sitting up begging for a treat. He sat up on his hind legs beside the kitchen table. His tongue was hanging out. His eyes were bright.

The second was Lucky sleeping warm and happy in front of the refrigerator. George stared at the two pictures. They blurred.

Coach Murray cleared his throat again. George gave the pictures one last look, then handed him the picture of Lucky in front of the refrigerator.

"We are in touch with the kennel and we'll let you know as soon as they find him."

Coach Murray turned and walked back out the door.

No one said a word. George sat on his bunk. He couldn't move.

One by one the other campers came up and patted George on the back.

"Sorry," said a boy named Tyler.

"Too bad," said a boy named John.

"I have a dog too," said Troy.

George didn't hear them. He was thinking about Lucky.

Lucky had escaped. Lucky was out somewhere alone.

A dog alone was in danger. Without George there to take care of him, Lucky could be run over by a car. Or attacked by bigger dogs. Or starve to death.

George closed his eyes. He still held one picture of Lucky.

He looked at it. He had to do something. He couldn't just sit here at camp while Lucky

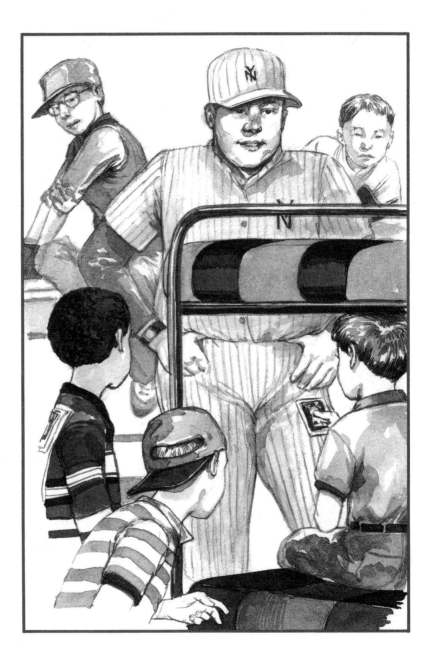

needed him. He had to find a way to help Lucky.

George looked around the cabin. It was empty. He didn't know how long he had been sitting on the bunk. He didn't care.

He reached under the pillow and took out his letter. He picked up his pencil and wrote one more line on the bottom.

P.S. Don't be afraid, Lucky. I'm coming to find you.

Escape!

I'm free! I'm free!

Lucky's feet beat a rhythm as he ran down the dirt road. He didn't look back. He didn't stop. He wouldn't stop until he was home. The wind blew in his face and it felt good. He was free.

He had used his escape trick. The one he had learned from his mother. He had licked the strange woman's hand as she carried him into the building. He had relaxed his body. He had pretended to be content even when he heard the sound of his family's station wagon driving away.

The sound meant that he had been left at this place, this place that must be the pound. He had been to the pound once and he had learned something there. That he never wanted to go back. He knew he had to escape.

He watched the woman and waited. He relaxed and licked. He waited until she made her mistake. She put him down to open the pen.

Lucky ran.

Darting back and forth he had avoided her grabbing hands and had slipped out the door and galloped down the road.

He had heard the barks of the other dogs as he slipped out.

YAAUU! WOOO! GRUFF!

He caught a glimpse of the other dogs as he ran out the door.

Ferocious dogs.

YAAUU. A basset hound howling with his nose pointed in the air.

WOOO. A sheep dog, brownish white fur standing out in all directions.

GRUFF. A Scottie, black as ink.

He heard the barks get softer and softer as he ran away. Away from the dogs. Away from the pound.

The woman had followed him at first. Lucky knew that she would. But he was faster.

Soon he heard her stop. Lucky heard her heavy breathing. She turned and headed back for the kennel.

He knew from his last trip to the pound what was next. Men would come looking for him. In a truck.

Lucky ran faster.

I'm free. I'm free.

His feet kept up the pace. His ears flapped in the wind. His tongue licked the air.

He came to a fork in the road. Now he was confused. He sniffed one road, then the other. Which road would take him home?

Before he could decide he heard the truck engine.

Lucky could tell just by the sound of an engine what kind of car it was.

A low, buzzing rumble that stopped and started, stopped and started, was the mail truck. A deep rumble with a loud screech and stop was the school bus. A medium buzz was the station wagon. This rumble was not the station wagon. This was the rumble of a truck.

He hurried over the side of the road and scooted into the tall grass. He crouched and watched. Yes, there was the truck. Behind the wheel he could see the woman.

She was driving slowly down the road with the window open. She was watching the side of the road.

Lucky crouched lower. He didn't want her to find him.

She called out the window as she drove.

"Here, boy. Here, Lucky."

Lucky crouched lower.

The truck came closer.

Lucky had the urge to dart out of the grass and run down the road. But he knew he shouldn't. He had to stay hidden. He had to stay quiet. He had to . . .

"Here, Lucky. Here, boy."

The woman was right beside him. Lucky whimpered softly.

She kept driving. She didn't see him. She took the left fork and kept on going.

The sound of the engine faded.

Lucky stood up and shook.

Now Lucky knew which way he needed to go. He could not go the same way as the woman. He looked down the road once at the disappearing truck and began to run down the other road.

The wind blew in his face and his feet beat a rhythm on the dirt road.

I'm free. I'm free.

Night Sounds

Dear Lucky,

It is the third day of camp. Five more minutes until lights out. Five more minutes until my escape! I should be on my way to find you soon.

You would have liked it here yesterday. We played baseball, baseball, and more baseball. I had hitting practice with Nix Brewer from the Cincinnati Reds. I slugged it into left field. I played third base. Nix says I'm going to be great. Wait until I show you how he taught me to throw. One little change in the wrist and the ball really flies.

We played against Cabin Nine. We have to play them every day. They beat us eleven to zip. They were not good winners.

I'm up to twenty-five mosquito bites.

Troy wet the bed again but he's a pretty good first baseman.

Lights out! Time for my escape!

I'm coming, Lucky, somehow.

Love,

George the Fearless

A trumpet sounded the lights-out signal. The counselor blew out the lanterns and left.

George folded the letter and put it under his pillow with the other letter to Lucky and his baseball cards. He felt around in the darkness for his flashlight. His hand found the cold metal of the handle and he grasped it. He slipped out of his sleeping bag and picked up his shoes. He would put them on outside where no one could hear him.

George made one last check. His flashlight, his jacket. He patted his back pocket, Lucky's picture, and his front pocket, his candy money. He would need the money to catch a bus. How do you catch a bus? He would figure it out later.

He tiptoed to the door.

He stepped outside and eased the screen door shut. The air was cool and the sky was clear. The moonlight was bright through the trees and George could see the path in front of him. All around him were the sounds of the forest.

Chirp. Buzz. Creak. Snap.

He shivered a little and sat down on the cabin steps to put on his tennis shoes. He tied the laces and sat for a minute listening to the night sounds. What was out there anyway?

He thought about Lucky, alone and needing him. He stood up and started down the path.

His feet crunched the gravel on the path. His flashlight swung long arcs of light in front of him. He would get to the camp entrance, then . . .

He hadn't thought this through very well. How could he get to town?

Crunch.

George snapped his head around and turned off his flashlight. He heard a low crunch on the path behind him.

He caught his breath and stood frozen in the darkness.

CRUNCH. Louder this time.

George backed slowly down the path. Something was there on the path. The something could be anything.

What animals live in the forest? He tried to remember. Bears, wolves, skunks . . .

CRUNCH!

George ran along the path in the darkness. As his feet crunched on the gravel, feet crunched on the gravel behind him. The crunching was getting closer and closer.

His foot hit a branch. George fell, tumbling down onto the path. The gravel dug into his palms. Bits of rock stuck to them. His knee dug into the rocks. His jeans ripped.

He rolled over. He held his flashlight up like a club. He would hit the attacker. The flashlight was all he had.

He turned it on and into the beam of the flashlight came . . .

Troy!

"George!" Troy said. "You okay? Where you going?"

George tried to catch his breath.

"Did I scare you?"

George didn't answer. He brushed the rocks from his palms and stood up. His legs were still shaky.

"What are you doing?" Troy asked.

"What are *you* doing?" George said. He noticed three rolls of toilet paper in Troy's hands.

"Well," Troy said slowly. He looked like he

was trying to decide whether or not to trust George.

Then he began to whisper. "I'm going to get Cabin Nine!"

"The ones that beat us today?"

"Yeah, I'm going to wrap their cabin in toilet paper!"

George giggled. He could imagine Cabin Nine waking up and finding their cabin wrapped in toilet paper.

"You want to come?" Troy handed a roll out to George.

George shook his head. He remembered Lucky.

"No," he said. "I was going to go find my dog."

Troy sighed. "I forgot," he said.

The two boys sat down on a log at the edge of the path.

"How are you going to do it?" asked Troy.

"I don't know," said George. "I thought I could just escape from camp and find him.

But it's too dark and I don't know how to get to town. It's hopeless."

Troy put his arm on George's shoulder.

"Let's go back," said Troy. The fun was gone from his voice. "I'll help you think of a plan."

The beams of their flashlights bounced up and down as they walked back to the cabin.

Troy stopped.

"I've got it," he said.

"What?"

"I know how you can get to town."

"How?"

"Every Wednesday Coach Murray drives into town for supplies. If you hide in the back of his car, you can hitch a ride. He'll never know."

George thought for a minute.

"Someone will miss me," he said.

"Don't worry," said Troy. "I'll cover for you."

George thought for a minute. It could

work. No one had missed him the first day when he had hidden during batting practice. And with Troy to cover for him—it had to work!

For the first time that week George smiled.

"Okay," he said. "Tomorrow—the great escape."

Troy smiled back. "But tonight," he said, "Cabin Nine?" He held out the roll of toilet paper to George.

George took the roll of toilet paper.

"Cabin Nine!" he answered as they ran back down the path toward Cabin Nine.

Moo, Bak Bak, Baa

Lucky got up from the ditch where he had spent the night and stretched. He had been traveling for a long time. He thought by now he would be home. He couldn't find his way.

There had been a little water in the ditch to drink but no food. He had not eaten since his escape.

His stomach growled. He thought about the dry dog food that he hated so much at home. For once he wished for a bowlful.

If he were home he would have breakfast. Then he would play ball with the boy. Then it would be time to chase the tabby cat next door. He missed the boy. He even missed the tabby cat.

MOO, BAK BAK, BAA.

He cocked his head and listened. There were strange noises coming from the other side of a row of bushes beside the road.

MOO, BAK BAK, BAA.

He listened again.

What could it be?

He scratched under the bushes. They were thick at the bottom. He crouched and scratched until he came through on the other side.

Lucky stopped and looked.

There was a house and a building beside it. Beside the building were some strange animals. Big animals. Animals that were eating grass and saying *MOO.*

He looked some more. Beside them were smaller animals. Animals eating grass and saying *BAAA.*

Lucky was not interested in these animals.

For one thing they were eating grass. They would not have any food that he could share. And another thing—they were too big to chase.

He was in the mood for a chase. Seeing other animals reminded him of how much he liked to chase the tabby cat.

BAK BAK.

Lucky's ears perked up. Beside the big animals were some fat birds pecking the ground and saying *BAK BAK*. They did not have any food to share. They were eating dirt. But they were just about the right size for a chase.

ERF!

Lucky charged forward. The birds scattered.

BAK BAK!

They called out and flapped their wings and flew in all directions.

Lucky wagged his tail. He picked out the biggest, fattest bird, a red one. He barked and chased her across the farmyard.

BAK BAK!

These animals were even more fun than the tabby cat!

Just as they would begin to land and settle on the ground he would charge forward again.

ERF! BAK BAK!

He almost caught one!

ERF! BAK BAK!

He would get that red one this time!

ERF! BAK BAK!

BANG!

Lucky cowered down when he heard the loud noise.

BANG! BANG!

The horrible noise again.

The birds were forgotten. This was the loudest noise that Lucky had ever heard. It hurt his ears. What was it?

He looked back at the house and saw a man coming toward him.

The man held a long shiny stick. A long shiny stick with smoke coming out of the end. As he watched, the man pulled up the long stick and pointed it at Lucky.

Lucky looked around the farmyard. There was no way out. He looked back at the man. The man was angry.

The man was stepping closer and closer.

Lucky tried to think.

What would his mother do?

She had taught him what to do when threatened. Body language. He had to show with his body who was boss.

To show who is boss he should stand up straight. Tail up. Head up. Eyes focused on the attacker. If the attacker came too close, he would raise the hair on his back and give a low growl.

There was another type of body language though. To show someone else that *they* are boss. To do this he should slump low, tuck his tail under his body, and lower his head. If the attacker came too close, he would roll over on his back, tummy up. It was embarrassing but it worked.

He looked at the man. The man was coming forward, stick in hand, close . . . closer . . . closer . . .

Lucky didn't need to think again.

He slumped low, tucked his tail, lowered his head, and rolled over on his back, tummy up.

SURRENDER!

The Great Escape

Dear Lucky,

I made it! I'm in the back of Coach Murray's car. In about half an hour he will drive to town. Then I can get out and take a bus to find you. Don't worry. I'll be there before night.

There's a baseball movie this afternoon—*Funniest Baseball Bloopers*. Troy will cover for me. They won't miss me until batting practice later this afternoon. By then I'll be on my way.

Nix might miss me at third. He

says I'm the best third baseman in the history of Camp Knockahoma. I think we might beat Cabin Nine today. We play them once every day. You should have seen their cabin this morning. Toilet paper was everywhere. Coach Murray stood out in front of the cabin calling out, "Move IT!" while they cleaned up.

All the boys in my cabin watched from the window. They're not so bad after all. Tyler is the best pitcher. His parents are biking in Europe. John plays second. This is his third year. Troy is my best friend though.

Tomorrow the whole camp will ride to Atlanta to see the Braves play the Dodgers. I won't be with them. I've never seen a pro game. But it's okay, Lucky. I won't let you down.

I'm coming!

Love,

George the Rescuer

George crouched low in the back of the car. It was hot and stuffy. The front door swung open and a cool breeze blew in. He took a breath but didn't move.

He heard Coach Murray get into the front seat. He heard the door slam shut and the engine start. With a bump the car moved forward. They were on their way.

George shifted his weight from his left to his right hip. His left leg was asleep. He wanted to stretch it out and wiggle his foot but he didn't dare.

The car bumped along. It hit one big bump and proceeded smoothly. George relaxed a little. They had made it to the highway.

George thought of the road signs that he had seen on his way to camp with his father. He pictured the signs telling the mileage in reverse:

DILLON   5 MILES

He wondered who would play third base

that afternoon. Could they beat Cabin Nine without him?

DILLON   10 MILES

He wondered about the Braves game. What would it be like? Would he ever get another chance to see a pro game?

DILLON   15 MILES

Soon they would be in town.

The car slowed down. George heard the blinker clink as they waited to turn.

The car eased forward and stopped moving. The engine stopped. They were probably at the store now. George would wait and give Coach Murray plenty of time to walk into the store.

He would count to one hundred. Then he would get out and make a run for it.

One . . . two . . . three . . .

A trickle of sweat dripped down his chin.

Forty-one . . . Forty-two . . . Forty-three . . .

He heard footsteps but he didn't pay attention. There were probably many cars in the parking lot.

Ninety-nine . . . One hundred!

George sat up and pulled on the door handle. The door swung open and he tumbled out onto the pavement—right beside two pinstriped legs in a Yankees uniform (too tight).

They were not at the store. Coach Murray had stopped for a newspaper. Coach Murray looked down at George. His mouth formed a perfect O of surprise.

George was caught.

Memories

Lucky lay on an old pink towel in the family room of the farmhouse. A man and a woman lived here.

His body language had worked. The man had not hurt him. He had picked Lucky up gently and scratched him and talked to him in a nice voice. He had brought Lucky in here, into the farmhouse.

Lucky was not hungry now. The man and woman had fed him a bowl of scraps from the table. Bits of bread and meat and rice covered with gravy.

He was not cold anymore. They had given him a warm spot beside the sofa in the family room.

He was not tired. He had slept long and deep all day on the towel.

He whimpered. He still was not happy.

It was not enough. Food and warmth and sleep were not enough.

He missed the boy.

Why didn't the boy want him anymore?

He did not know. He thought back over their life together. What could have gone wrong?

Was it the time that he had barked in the backyard when he was a puppy? He had only barked long enough to show them that he wanted to sleep in the house. He had only barked long enough to make the boy come outside to sleep with him in the doghouse. That couldn't be it. Or could it?

There was that other time. When he was young. He had been left in the station wagon.

They had left a brown paper bag with ham in it in the back of the station wagon. He had chewed, just a tiny bit, on the bag. Only a few groceries had scattered about. Yes, there was that puddle he had made when they found him. But he had been so nervous. Surely it wasn't that time. Or was it?

Could it have been the time he chewed on Mrs. Haines's Japanese dogwoods?

Or the briefcase?

Or the baseball glove?

Had he chased the tabby cat too many times?

Perhaps they had discovered the small puddle he had made behind the sofa last week when no one would let him out.

Lucky's head felt heavy. He didn't lift it. He didn't get up. He didn't want to do anything. He just wanted his boy to forgive him. He just wanted to go home.

The woman walked into the room.

"Poor old Sport," she said. She bent down

and scratched him on the chest. She put a small piece of ham beside his nose.

Lucky didn't move.

Even ham didn't smell good today.

Psst!

Dear Lucky,

I failed! Coach Murray nabbed me. It was a frightening sight. A middle-aged man in a Yankees uniform staring at me. His face was so surprised.

I thought he would yell. He didn't. I thought he would be mad. He wasn't. I thought he would make me go back to camp. He did.

It's almost time for lights out. I won't be coming today.

Tomorrow we go to Atlanta for the Braves game. We leave first thing in the morning. Coach will be watching me. I don't know what I can do. I don't know how I can save you. Be strong, Lucky. I'm sorry I let you down.

Love,

George the Failure

A lone trumpet sounded taps and the lanterns were blown out.

George lay in the darkness. He held Lucky's picture. It was too dark to see it. As he rubbed his fingers over the picture he could see in his mind a little dog standing on his hind legs, tongue out, eyes bright. He blinked and let a tear roll down his cheek. No one could see him cry in the dark.

Psst.

He heard Troy call him.

He didn't answer.

Psst.

He heard him again.

Still he didn't answer. There was no hope now.

Troy's flashlight came on. The beam swung in an arc across the room and down to his bunk as Troy climbed down. Troy arranged a blanket on each side of the bunk beds so that no one could see the light.

"Now," said Troy. "We need a plan."

George shook his head. "There's no way," he said.

PSST!

A noise came from outside the blanket. Troy pulled it back and let Tyler crawl under.

PSST!

Under came John. Then the rest of the boys. Soon there were nine boys on George's bunk bed.

"We need a plan," said Troy. "We need a plan to rescue George's dog, Lucky."

"I've got it," John said. "It's lights out. We can take our flashlights and sneak out down the—"

"Won't work," said Troy. He looked at George and smiled.

"It's been tried."

"Oh," said John.

"I know," said Tyler. "Someone can hide in the back of Coach Murray's car and—"

"Won't work," said George.

"It's been tried?"

"Yes," said Troy.

"Oh," said all the boys together.

They sat in silence for a moment.

"What's that?" said Troy. He pointed to the picture that George was holding.

"Lucky's picture," said George. His voice cracked.

Troy took the picture.

It was wrinkled on the edges. Lucky still looked out from the picture. Standing on his hind legs.

The boys stared at the picture in silence.

"If only we had a way to show this picture to people—lots of people," said Troy.

Troy leaned back against the bars of the bunk bed.

"But how can we do that? We are stuck here in camp miles away from any people."

George sat up. "Troy," he said, "you've got it!"

He reached out and took the picture back. He smiled. He held the picture up. "This," he said, "is the answer. This picture will save Lucky."

There was silence for a moment. Then George began to speak. Afterward it was a long time before anyone in Cabin Eight got to sleep.

Nine boys looked through their things to find the supplies they would need.

John pulled an extra sheet out from his trunk.

"How's this?" he asked George.

"Perfect!"

Tyler took out a set of poster paints from his suitcase. "We can use these," he said.

"Perfect!"

Troy brought out a large canvas gym bag.

"We can hide everything in this," he said.

"Perfect!"

The next morning George made his bed

without a single complaint. He cleaned the lanterns and washed the dishes after breakfast.

The bus to Atlanta pulled up to the dining hall and honked the horn. All the campers boarded the bus.

Cabin Eight boarded the bus and no one noticed the large canvas gym bag that George carried.

Cabin Eight had a plan.

TV Sounds

Lucky lay in front of the TV. He watched the man and woman. They sat on the sofa and stared at the flickering screen. Lucky had never understood exactly what the TV was.

His boy would watch it sometimes and would laugh or stare at it.

Sounds came out of it. Talking, strange laughter, sirens, motor sounds, and sometimes barks.

Today the sounds were baseball sounds. Cheers from a crowd of people and the crack of bats. Lucky whined. The sounds made him even sadder. They made him remember the boy.

"Go, Braves!" the man yelled.

He remembered his baseball games with the boy. The boy let him play left field. He loved baseball.

CRACK! He heard the crack of a bat from the TV and remembered what it felt like to run for the ball with the boy. The boy would call "Get it, Lucky!" or "Good dog, Lucky!"

He hadn't heard his name for a long time.

He missed the sound of his name.

"What's the matter, Sport?" said the woman. She scratched him a little with her foot. She didn't scratch him the way the boy did.

SPORT? Why did she keep saying that word?

The man's eyes were focused on the TV. He said baseball words like *Comeon comeon comeon!*

GET IT! GET IT!

As he said each "Get it!" he would rise a

little higher from his seat until the last "Get it!" when he stood and raised his fists in the air.

When he did this Lucky barked.

"Quiet, Sport," said the woman.

Sport? There was that name again.

Name!

Lucky looked at the woman. Now he had figured it out. She had changed his name.

If this was his new name, then this was his new home.

The woman rubbed his back one more time.

Lucky settled back down on the towel to think.

His new home. There were good things about this home. The food was good. The people were nice. The chickens were fun to chase.

But there were things that he would miss. His rubber newspaper that the boy always threw for him. The bone that he had buried in his special hiding place under the pecan tree.

Playing left field in the boy's baseball games. And the boy.

Without warning the woman jumped up.

The man jumped up too.

They ran back and forth across the room.

Lucky stood up and barked. Something must be happening on the TV. Something exciting.

The woman called out something to the man. He ran into the kitchen and came back with a pencil and paper.

The man hurried over to the telephone and began to dial. The woman turned to Lucky and stooped down beside him. She petted him gently on the head.

When she spoke Lucky knew that everything was going to be all right. She had said the most welcome word in the human language. It was the word he had missed hearing the most throughout this long week.

"Lucky!" she said.

Lost Dog

The Braves were in the field. The Dodgers were up to bat. But George and Troy were not watching the game. At that moment no one was watching the game.

The TV cameraman had focused the camera on the small picture that George held up. The TV picture was projected on the giant screen above the scoreboard. The TV picture was projected to thousands of homes.

Everyone was watching the scoreboard. Flashing on the giant screen above the scoreboard was the picture of a small furry dog sitting up begging, tongue out, eyes bright.

Lucky.

The crowd let out a long sigh.

AWWWWWWW!

Then the cameraman focused on the large banner that the boys of Cabin Eight held up and a picture of the banner flashed on the screen. The camera focused closer and the words became clear:

LOST DOG   NAME: LUCKY
LOST IN THE LaGRANGE AREA
IF YOU FIND THIS DOG PLEASE CALL MRS. MINNIE AT
555-8976

The boys of Cabin Eight were hoarse. They had yelled their loudest. They had jumped up and down waving the banner. It had taken three innings but finally they caught the attention of the cameraman and the camera zeroed in.

George held up the picture and one end of the banner. Troy held up the other end. The other boys held up the banner across the middle.

And the message went out.

The cameraman focused the camera back on the field. The boys sat down to watch the game. They had done it.

Coach Murray smiled at George. George crossed his fingers. This was the best that he could do. Now he could only wait.

Would it work? Had someone found Lucky? Would the person who had found Lucky be watching the game on TV? Thousands of people were watching. George hoped it would work.

He sat back. The Braves made the last out and ran in from the field.

Before the first batter could come to the plate a cheer rose up from the crowd.

Troy grabbed George's arm. "Look!" he yelled. "Look!"

George looked up at the electronic scoreboard.

On the board was a message:

LUCKY HAS BEEN FOUND!

The message flashed over and over.

The crowd clapped and cheered. Cabin Eight clapped and cheered. Coach Murray clapped and cheered.

Whoever had found Lucky had called Mrs. Minnie. Mrs. Minnie had called the stadium. Lucky had been found.

Going Home?

Before Lucky knew what had happened he was back at Mrs. Minnie's Kennel. Back with the barking dogs.

YAAUU! WOO! GRUFF!

Lucky looked out at the other pens.

YAAUU!

The large brown and black basset hound in the pen across from Lucky didn't sound very happy. When he howled he held his head straight up with his nose pointed at the ceiling.

WOOOO!

The brownish white sheep dog in the third pen down sounded even less happy. He bent his head down to howl and rocked his body side to side.

GRUFF!

The small black Scottie in the pen beside the door was the saddest of all. He was lying down on his side in the pen. He didn't even get up to howl. When it was his turn he just lifted his head a little off the cedar chips and barked.

Lucky realized something now. These dogs were not barking at him. These dogs felt just like he did. They were here away from their homes like him. Their masters didn't want them either.

Lucky knew just how they were feeling. He lifted up his head.

When the howls began again, he added his misery howl.

YAAUU! WOOOO! GRUFF!
AAAAAOOOOOOOOOOOOOO!
BANG!

In walked the woman. But this time she was not alone.

Behind her, hurrying through the door, came three small girls.

They were squealing with delight. "Mac-Duff! MacDuff!" they called out.

GGGRRRUUUFFFF!

The Scottie jumped up and barked a happy, excited bark. The woman opened the door of his pen.

Lucky pressed his nose tightly against the bars. This was not in the routine! This was better than the routine!

The Scottie ran out of his pen to the girls. His back legs hopped double time with excitement.

On the floor of the kennel was a pile of three girls and one Scottie. A pile of pats and gruffs and licks and laughter.

Lucky pressed even closer.

Something new had happened today. Something amazing. Something wonderful.

Something that had *never* happened at the pound!

The Scottie's family had come back!

In the distance Lucky could hear the rumble of an engine. He cocked his head and listened. This rumble was not just any engine, this rumble was the medium buzz from his people's station wagon.

These three girls had come back for their dog. He hardly dared to hope that *his* family was coming back for him. But he did hope.

ERF! ERF!

He barked his loudest bark. He danced back and forth on his four paws excitedly. The rumble got louder.

ERF! ERF!

He dared to hope.

The engine stopped.

Lucky was quiet now. He trembled. Was it them?

BANG!

The door flew open. In ran the boy, HIS BOY!

With one quick motion the boy opened the pen and Lucky ran out to him. One jump and he was in the boy's arms. He was overcome by the smell of the boy and the strong feeling of the boy's arms.

Never had he been so happy. He licked the boy's face to the left and the right and the center. The boy was turning his face away to avoid the licks. Lucky couldn't help himself. He licked anyway.

It was a happy day for Lucky. He was going home.

Dear Troy

George rode in the backseat of the station wagon. Lucky's head rested on his lap. Lucky's eyes were closed. He was asleep.

George patted Lucky on his back. His fur was warm and sleek.

The last day of camp had passed quickly. He had known that Lucky was safe back at Mrs. Minnie's. He had had a wonderful time.

George's father was driving. George could see the suntanned back of his neck. George's mother was telling about a lobster his father had caught while they were snorkeling. They were both laughing.

His mother went on with her story but George had stopped listening. He was remembering camp.

He looked down at Lucky asleep in his lap.

A part of him had hurt all week missing Lucky. But he would not have wanted to miss out on camp either. He was already missing Cabin Eight and Troy and Coach Murray. He would never forget the night he and Troy wrapped Cabin Nine in toilet paper. Or the night that nine boys had a meeting on his bed and made the plan to save Lucky. Or the last day when Cabin Eight had finally beaten Cabin Nine seven to six.

Lucky stretched a little on his lap.

George sighed. No matter what you did there would always be something to miss.

From the front seat came more laughter.

Now George could picture his parents on the sailboat, swimming and snorkeling. George could even picture them on the sailboat missing him.

He rested his head back on the car seat. It

had been a long trip. Lucky stretched out a little on his lap.

He reached down to rub Lucky one more time. In his pocket he had the packet of letters to Lucky. Writing the letters had helped him not to miss Lucky so much. It gave him an idea. He took his white tablet from his tote bag and started another letter. But this one had a different beginning.

Dear Troy,

About the author

Betsy Duffey was born in Anderson, South Carolina, and was graduated from Clemson University. The character Lucky was inspired by her dog, Chester, and the ten other dogs her family has owned over the years.

Betsy Duffey lives with her husband and two sons in Atlanta, Georgia.

About the illustrator

Leslie Morrill has illustrated many books for children. He lives in Chevy Chase, Maryland.